ISLAND SUMMER

Catherine Stock

Lothrop, Lee & Shepard Books
New York

For my summery friends Reidar, Ingerd, Christina,
Maria, Antonio, Calypso, Paniotis, Caterina, Nicos,
Flora, Evangelina, Giorgio, Pablo, and Bertrand

Pencil and watercolors were used for the full-color illustrations.
The text type is 16-point Stone Serif.
Copyright © 1999 by Catherine Stock

Published by Lothrop, Lee & Shepard Books
a division of William Morrow and Company, Inc.
1350 Avenue of the Americas, New York, NY 10019
www.williammorrow.com

Printed in Hong Kong by South China Printing Company (1988) Ltd.

10 9 8 7 6 5 4 3 2 1

Library of Congress Cataloging-in-Publication Data

Stock, Catherine.
Island summer/Catherine Stock.
p. cm.
Summary: Summer transforms a quiet island as visitors arrive for swimming,
playing on the beach, card games, soccer, hide-and-seek,
and dancing in the evening.
ISBN 0-688-12780-0 (trade)—ISBN 0-688-12781-9 (library)
[1. Islands—Fiction. 2. Summer—Fiction.] I. Title.
PZ7.S8635Is 1999 [E]—dc21 98-46401 CIP AC

The little island lies alone in the sea.

In the winter everything is gray and closed and cold. The village houses huddle around the bay like pale pebbles, afraid that the winter storms will grab them up and toss them far out into the sea.

The wet wind swirls crusty brown leaves down the valley and through the empty alleyways, looking for a loose shutter to pry open and bang.

Then, slowly, the sun grows stronger, squeezing the wild wind into a soft spring breeze. It soothes the angry waves into a flat, shimmering sea and soaks up the muddy puddles like freshly baked pound cake sops up melted chocolate.

The little village, fresh and sparkling in the warm spring sunshine, waits.

But not for long: Here comes the little ferryboat, putt, putt, putting into the bay with a loud, long whistle. Out tumble the people from the mainland, loaded down with baskets and bags and brooms and boxes.

Into the village they march to throw open doors and shutters and windows. Out come the mattresses to air, the blankets to beat, the tables to scrub. There's so much to do before the summer people come!

At last, after three days of hard work, the little village is ready.

And here they are: the ladies with their hats and cats and sun umbrellas, the men with their folding chairs and playing cards and newspapers . . .

and the children with their buckets and beach balls and snorkels and flippers and all their noisy noisy noise. They run and chase and hide-and-seek one another all over the village and up and down the beach.

It's summertime at last and everyone has burst out of school and work and winter. Oh, how nice to throw on cotton shirts and baggy pants and pad around on bare brown feet and in flappy flip-flop sandals.

At midday the sun shines hot and everyone squabbles and whines: *It's my turn in the hammock. . . . Give me back my snorkel. . . . Why can't we swim after lunch?*

Finally the heat melts all the grumbles into sleep,
until the only sound left is the buzzing of a fat
black fly making lazy circles in the shade of an
olive tree.

No one can hold a grudge for long. By late
afternoon even the losing soccer team is okay, once
they've thrown the winning team into the water
and rubbed sand in their hair.

Children shuffle their dominoes while the men
smack down their cards. The women are somewhere
showering, and scenting their hair.

It's midsummer. New friends meet one another
and old friends greet one another. The fiddler
tightens up his bow, and the dancing begins.

And when the moon is full and round and white, midnight swimmers tiptoe past slumbering parents, down to the water for a skinny dip.

Like sand trickling through fingers, the summer months thin into weeks, then days, then hours. The summer people scribble quick postcards home and scramble for souvenirs to tuck into their knapsacks.

Then come the last swims, the last hugs, the last sighs.

And the summer people are gone.

The people from the mainland tidy up the houses, shutter the windows, and bolt the doors. They stretch their tired backs and help one another onto the little ferryboat.

With one last long whistle, the boat chugs out of the bay. They are all gone.

Quiet and still, the village remains. The island settles down for the long winter months ahead, alone once again in the sea.